Eva Eland

WHERE HAPPINESS BEGINS

Random House 🏠 New York

Are you looking for Happiness?

It often has disguises and
goes by different names.

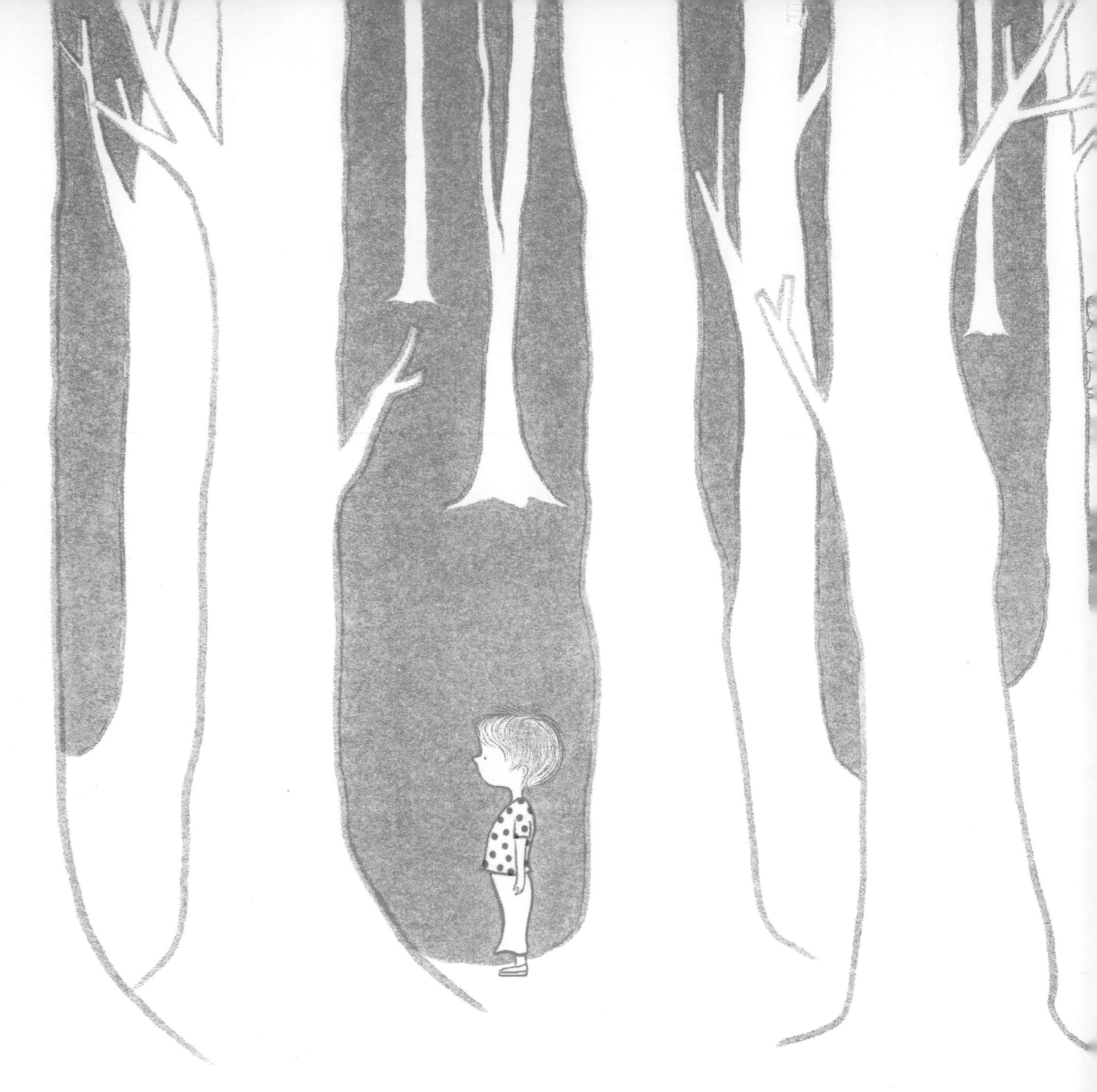

Some days it seems to be hiding,

while on others,
it's right there with you
wherever you go.

You can try to
understand it,

collect it,

or protect it.

You can try to catch it. . . .

But most of
the time
Happiness
appears to
have a will
of its own.

And sometimes it may feel as if there are too many things that get between you and Happiness.

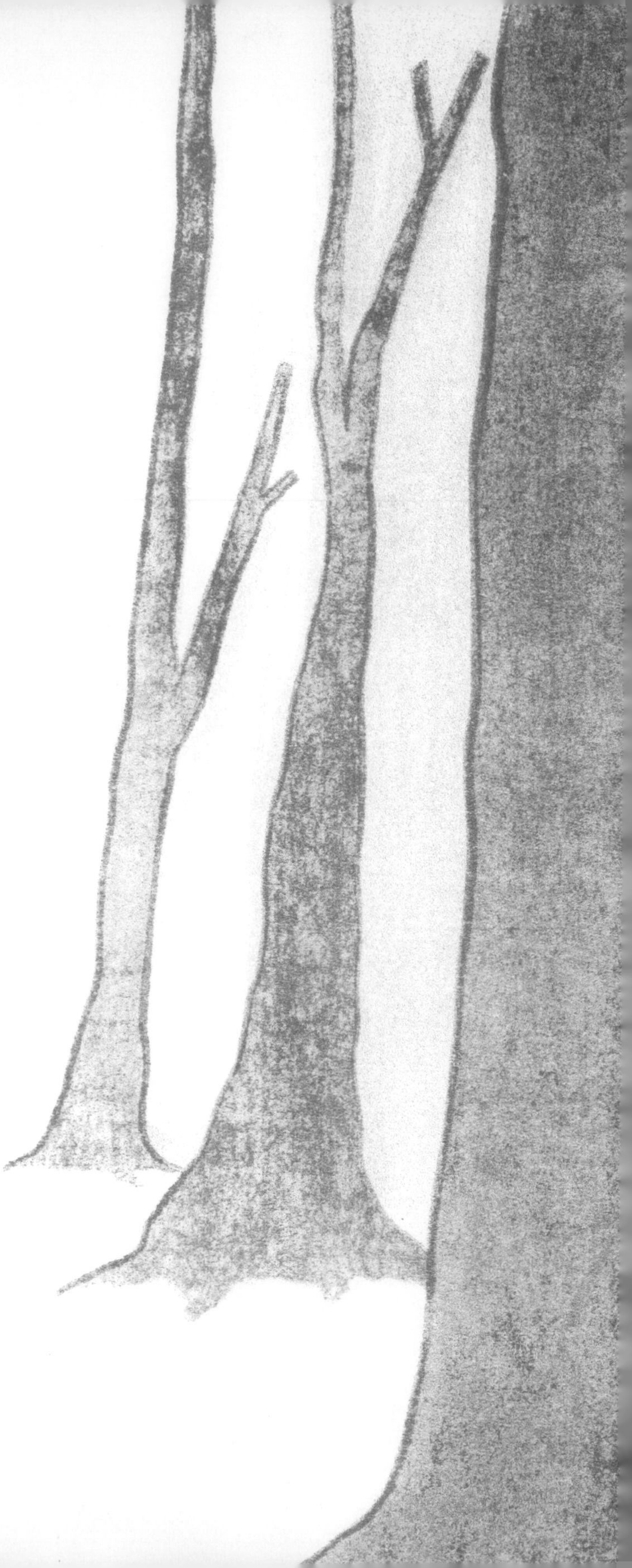

It's not always easy, but when
you find your way through,

Happiness will
be there,
waiting.

When you do find it,
start following—see
where it will take you.

Happiness may be different
from what you expect, or
feel a little scary at first,

but it will let you
find new paths,
enjoy your time with
family and friends,
and do the things
you love to do.

You can't feel happy
all the time. You might feel
overwhelmed by your feelings
and that you can't always control them,
but you can find your way back home.

Just breathe. . . .

In that quiet moment
you will realize you
don't have to keep
looking for Happiness....

It was always there.
Recognize it and treasure it
because, in the end,
Happiness begins with you.

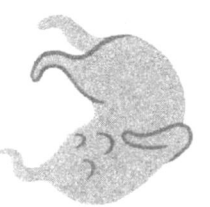